EGMONT

We bring stories to life

This edition published in Great Britain 2008 by Dean
an imprint of Egmont UK Limited
239 Kensington High Street, London W8 6SA
© 2008 Disney Enterprises, Inc
Based on the Winnie-the-Pooh works by A. A. Milne and E. H. Shepard
Illustrations by Andrew Grey
Text by Jude Exley

ISBN 978 0 6035 6361 4
1 3 5 7 9 10 8 6 4 2
Printed in China

All About

Tigger

This book belongs to . . .

Meet Tigger

Here is Tigger, ready to be introduced to you.
He may be bouncing rather a lot, but that is because
he is very excited to meet you. As you may know,
Tigger is a very bouncy animal and a very

Friendly Tigger.

In this book you will learn all about the strange
animal called Tigger, including what he really likes
to eat for breakfast. And you
can listen to a story about
Tigger — a bouncy story.
Because Tigger does rather
a lot of that . . .

A Poem about Tigger

He came to the Forest late one night,

The noise was enough to give Pooh a fright.

"Worraworraworra," he said,

And Pooh got out of bed,

To find a Bouncy Tigger ahead.

Tigger now lives with Kanga and Roo,

Eating enough Medicine for two!

Never was an animal bouncier than he,

(Except when he was stuck up a tree.)

A Friendlier Tigger there never will be!

Facts about Tigger

He came to the Forest late one night. Pooh had never seen a Tigger before, and Tigger didn't know what he liked, but they were both friends with Christopher Robin.

He lives with Kanga and Roo in a different part of the Forest from Pooh. There is a very good reason why he lives with them, which will soon become clear.

He likes Extract of Malt – Roo's Strengthening Medicine. He has it for breakfast, dinner and tea. That's why he lives at Kanga's house!

🍾 *He doesn't climb trees.* Tigger thought that he did, but when he started to climb, he realised his tail got in the way and he needed help to get back down.

🍾 *He is very bouncy.* So bouncy in fact, that he bounced Eeyore into the river, and Pooh thought that he was Piglet's stick in a game of Poohsticks.

🍾 *He never gets lost.* He bounces and runs round in circles, squares and up and down, but Tigger never gets lost. Tiggers just don't, as Rabbit found out.

He is a Friendly Tigger. He is great friends with little Roo who he could play with all day. And when Rabbit is lost in the Forest, Tigger goes to find him.

He makes lots of unusual noises. When Tigger arrived at Pooh's house, he said "Worraworraworraworraworra" and he coughed "Grr-oppp-ptschschschz" when Eeyore bounced into the river.

He is the only Tigger. Well, he thinks he is, and is very surprised when he finds somebody just like him in the mirror.

In which we read about

Tigger

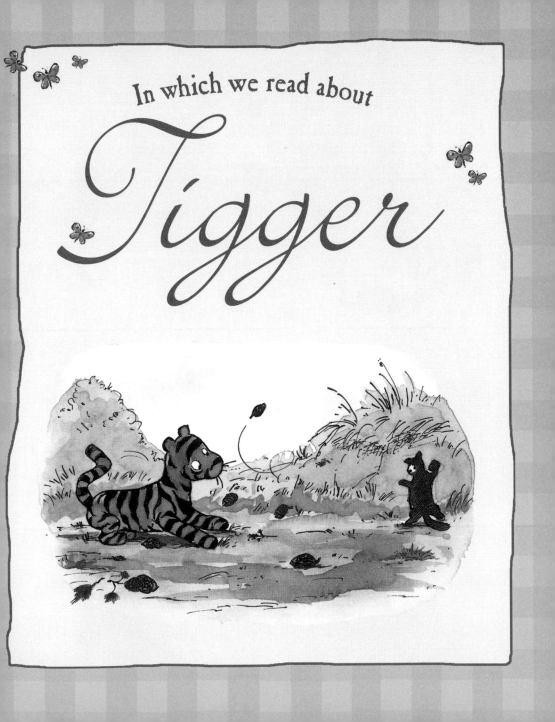

One night Pooh woke up suddenly when he thought he heard somebody trying to get into his honey cupboard. He got out of bed, but there was no one there. There was just a strange noise. There are lots of noises in the Forest, but this was different. It wasn't a growl

or a purr,

or a squeak,

or a neigh,

like Piglet or Eeyore might make, it was a

"Worrdworrdworrdworrd".

Pooh decided to ask the strange animal making that noise not to do it again. He opened his front door and said "hello".

The strange animal introduced himself as Tigger. Pooh had never seen a Tigger before, but he was very pleased to hear that he was a friend of Christopher Robin's and invited him in.

"Do Tiggers like honey?" asked Pooh.

"Tiggers like everything," said Tigger, happily. And they both went to sleep.

The next morning,
Pooh woke up to
see Tigger looking
at himself in
the mirror.

"I thought I was the only one," said Tigger, "but
I've just met someone like me!"

Then suddenly Tigger jumped at Pooh's
tablecloth and with a loud

"Worrdworrdworrdworrdworrd",

he pulled it off the table and rolled across
the room with it.

"Did I win?" he asked, cheerfully.

"That's my tablecloth," replied Pooh, putting the
cloth and two pots of honey on the table.

They both sat down to breakfast and Tigger
helped himself to a large mouthful of honey, making
exploring movements with his tongue ...
and "what-is-this noises"? ...
and then he said:
"Tiggers don't like honey."
"I thought they liked everything," said Pooh,
trying to sound disappointed, but actually feeling
very pleased – particularly when Tigger said that

they liked
everything
except honey.

So Pooh took Tigger to Piglet's house.
Piglet had never seen a Tigger before and he was
a little bit scared. But Pooh explained that Tigger
would like some haycorns for breakfast and
Piglet said, "Help yourself".

When Tigger had a mouthful of haycorns,
he said
"Ee-ers o i a-ors"
and then
"skoos ee",
before saying firmly:
"Tiggers don't like
haycorns."

Piglet was rather glad and asked if he liked thistles
instead, and Tigger said that was what he liked best.

Then the three of them went to the part of the Forest where Eeyore lived. Eeyore was a little unsure of Tigger at first, and asked what he was and when he was going. But when Pooh explained that he was a friend of Christopher Robin's who wanted some thistles for breakfast, Eeyore showed him to a very thistly looking patch of thistles.

Tigger wasn't sure that these really were
the thistles that Tiggers like best, but he took
a large, crunchy mouthful.

"Ow! Hot!" said Tigger, putting his paw in his
mouth and shaking his head to get the prickles out.

Eeyore thought that Tigger had eaten a bee, but
Tigger, running round in circles with his tongue
hanging out, explained that Tiggers don't like thistles.

Pooh was very confused. Tiggers didn't like honey, haycorns or thistles. Maybe Christopher Robin could help? So they went to find Christopher Robin, with Tigger bouncing in front of them, turning round every now and then to check that this was the right way.

Soon Tigger saw Christopher Robin, and rushed up to him.

"Oh, there you are, Tigger!" said Christopher Robin.

Pooh asked Christopher Robin what Tiggers
like to eat for breakfast, but he didn't know either.
He thought Kanga would be able to help. So they
all went to Kanga's house.

Pooh was very
pleased to find some
condensed milk
in her cupboard.
But Tigger put his
nose into this and
his paw into that,
and he still couldn't
find anything that
Tiggers like.

Then he saw Kanga trying to give Roo his
Strengthening Medicine. Roo was trying
his best not to have it, when Tigger suddenly
put out his tongue and the Extract of Malt
medicine went straight into Tigger's mouth.

"Tigger, dear!" said Kanga.

"He's taken my medicine!" sang Roo happily.

Then Tigger closed his eyes, moved his tongue
round and round, and with a happy smile on his
face said, "So, that's what Tiggers like!"

Everyone was very happy to know finally what
Tiggers like. And from then on, it was decided that
Tigger would live at Kanga's house, so he could eat
Extract of Malt for breakfast, dinner and tea. And
sometimes as **Strengthening Medicine**, too.

A few days later, Kanga was beginning to realise
that there were times when a bouncy animal like
Tigger shouldn't be in the house. So she sent
Tigger and Roo out to have a nice long morning
in the Forest, not getting into mischief.

Tigger was telling Roo about all the things Tiggers
can do. Roo was very excited
to learn that climbing trees
is what Tiggers do best.

So Roo sat on Tigger's
back and Tigger began to
climb a very tall tree.
It was going well, until . . .
Snap! . . .
the branch he was standing on broke . . .
and Tigger had to climb quickly on to
the one above it. Roo was having lots
of fun and he couldn't wait to go higher,
but Tigger told him that he didn't want
to go higher and his tail got in the
way if he tried to climb down.

Just then, Pooh and Piglet came along.

"Hallo, Roo," called Piglet. "What are you doing?"

"We can't get down!" cried Roo. "Isn't it fun?
Tigger and I are living in a tree, just like Owl."

Pooh and Piglet didn't know how to get them
down either. Luckily, Christopher Robin came
strolling along, and decided that he would take off
his tunic, so they could hold it out under the tree
for Roo and Tigger to jump into.

Roo was wildly excited, and he jumped straight
into the tunic, bouncing back up into the air when
he landed, and saying "Oo, lovely!" for a while.

Tigger was less sure. He was holding on to the
branch nervously, until suddenly, with a crash
and a tearing noise, Tigger flew past the tree
and landed in a heap with everyone on the ground.
They all picked themselves up and Tigger bounced
happily away with little Roo.

After a while, some of the animals in the Forest
began to get annoyed by Tigger's bounciness.

One sunny day, Rabbit was talking to Pooh
and Piglet about teaching Tigger a lesson. Piglet
agreed that however much you liked Tigger, it was
a very good idea to think of a way of **unbouncing**
him. But he wasn't sure how they should do it.
And Pooh was humming to himself, so it was left
to Rabbit to come up with an idea.

Rabbit decided that they would take Tigger
exploring to the North Pole and lose him there,
so that by the time he found his way home,
he would be a very different Tigger altogether.
Pooh was glad that they were going to the
North Pole, as Tigger would see the sign that

said Pooh found it

and then he would

know what sort

of bear he was.

DICScoVERED By
PooH
PooH FouND IT

The next morning, it was cold and misty. Piglet was worried about how miserable it would be for Tigger to be lost on a day like this. But Rabbit thought it was the perfect weather, as when Tigger bounced out of sight, they could hide and he wouldn't be able to see them.

"Not never?" said Piglet, worriedly.

"Well, not until we find him again," said Rabbit.

At Kanga's house, Tigger and Roo were very
pleased to see their friends and very excited at the
thought of an adventure. But Rabbit didn't think
Tigger's good friend Roo should come along.

"He was coughing earlier," he said to Kanga.

"It was just a biscuit cough," said Roo.

"Oh, Roo dear," said Kanga.

"You can go
another day."
And it was
decided that
he would
stay at
home.

So, off they went. Pooh, Rabbit and Piglet walked together, with Tigger running around them in circles, squares, and when the bushes got prickly, up and down in front of them. He kept **bouncing** into Rabbit and then disappearing in the mist.

Rabbit decided that now was the right time. He jumped into a gap beside the path and Pooh and Piglet followed him.

The Forest was silent. Then they heard Tigger say:
"hello?"
They all waited silently until they heard him wander
off. Piglet felt very brave. When they were sure he had
left, and they were all beginning to get a bit scared in
the dark gap, they hurried off, with Rabbit leading
the way home.

"Why are we going this way?" asked Pooh.

"I thought we went right," said Piglet, nervously.

But Rabbit was sure he knew the way, and half an hour later, he kept saying,

"here we are," and

"no, we're not."

And then,

"it's lucky I know the Forest so well, or we might get lost."

Tigger waited for the others to catch him
up, but when he got tired of waiting, he went
home. Kanga was waiting for him with his
Strengthening Medicine.

Just as they finished dinner,
Christopher Robin arrived.
He soon realised that Pooh,
Piglet and Rabbit were
lost in the Forest.

"Tiggers never
get lost," whispered
Tigger to Roo.

Christopher Robin
asked Tigger to help
him find them and
off they went.

Rabbit, Pooh and Piglet were having a rest
in a sand pit that they seemed to keep ending
up in. Pooh was sure that his honey pots were
calling him, but he couldn't hear them because
Rabbit kept talking. So Pooh persuaded Rabbit
to set off again by himself. Rabbit walked into the
mist, and after twenty minutes, Pooh and Piglet
walked off together.

Just when Pooh and Piglet began to know where they were, out of the mist came Christopher Robin.

"Oh, there you are," he said carelessly, trying to pretend he wasn't worried. "Tigger will find Rabbit. He's sort of looking for you all."

"We are just going home for a little something," said Pooh, and Christopher Robin decided to go home with them.

Meanwhile, Tigger was bouncing around the Forest, making loud yapping noises, looking for Rabbit.

At last, a very small and sorry Rabbit heard him. And he rushed to the noise to discover that it was a Friendly Tigger, who bounced in just the way a Tigger **should** bounce.

"Oh, Tigger, I am very glad to see you," he cried happily. And off they went home together.